CASHEW edible
O-roy

CHILI edible
Pom-wa

Sap of tree—for skin infections
Wah-kah-pwe-mah

U-shuh

for fevers
Pah-ke-rah-shwe

for fevers
Kah-pi-ah-me

WATER LILY

for fevers
She-tu-u-ru

Inner bark sap—for skin fungus
Wee-dee

TONKA BEAN for fevers
O-to

VANILLA edible

TOBACCO for rheumatism
Tih-kuh

Kah-lo-she-wah for childbirth

for hexes and fevers
Mah-tu-kru

WILD PEPPER for toothaches

Kah-pi ah-wah-rah for strength

Kru-ku-ne for cuts

Ah-puh-muh tih-kuh

for good luck

Go-lo-be (fungus) for earaches

PLANTS OF THE SURINAME RAIN FOREST

ENGLISH PLANT NAMES ARE IN CAPITAL LETTERS.

Phonetic spellings are from the Tirio language.

Many Amazonian plants do not have English names.

THE SHAMAN'S APPRENTICE

A TALE OF THE AMAZON RAIN FOREST

WRITTEN BY

Lynne Cherry and
Mark J. Plotkin

Illustrated by Lynne Cherry

A GULLIVER GREEN BOOK

HARCOURT BRACE & COMPANY

San Diego   New York   London

Library of Congress Cataloging-in-Publication Data
Cherry, Lynne.
The shaman's apprentice: a tale of the Amazon rain forest/written by
Lynne Cherry and Mark J. Plotkin; illustrated by Lynne Cherry.
p.   cm.
"Gulliver Green."
Summary: Kamanya believes in the shaman's wisdom about the
healing properties of plants found in the Amazon rain forest and
hopes one day to be a healer for his people.
ISBN 0-15-201281-8
[1. Healers—Fiction.   2. Rain forests—Amazon River Region—
Fiction.   3. Amazon River Region—Fiction.]
I. Cherry, Lynne.   II. Plotkin, Mark J.   III. Title.
PZ7.P7235Sh   1998
[E]—dc21   97-5978

I H G F E D C B A

Printed in Singapore

Gulliver Green® books focus on various aspects of ecology and the
environment, and a portion of the proceeds from the sale of these
books is donated to protect, preserve, and restore native forests.

The paintings in this book were done in Pentel watercolors
on Strathmore 400 watercolor paper.
The display type is a hand-altered version of Herculanum.
The text type was set in Columbus.
Color separations by Bright Arts, Ltd., Singapore
Printed and bound by Tien Wah Press, Singapore
This book was printed on totally chlorine-free Nymolla
Matte Art paper.
Production supervision by Stanley Redfern and Ginger Boyer
Designed by Linda Lockowitz

Our thanks to all the wonderful people of Kwamala and especially
to the following: Isaac, who modeled for the shaman's apprentice
as a child; Kamanya, who modeled for the shaman's apprentice as
a grown man; Nahtahlah, the medicine man, who modeled for the
shaman and who shared his wisdom of the rain forest with both
Lynne and Mark; Koita, who modeled for the chief; Amasina,
Yaloefah, and the other people of Kwamala who modeled for the
Tirio villagers; Liliana Madrigal, who posed as the ethnobotanist;
R. E. Schultes; Judi and Henk Reichart, Chris Healy, Neville Gunther,
Marga Werkhoven, Iwan Derfeld, and Gum Air for logistical support
in Suriname; and to our beloved Frits Von Troon, who continues to
serve as guide, teacher, mentor, and friend.

Lynne Cherry wishes to thank the Marine Biological Laboratory,
Woods Hole, Massachusetts, for her artist-in-residency.

To the memories of
two great conservationists:
Al Gentry and Ted Parker,
whose expertise and dedication
continue to inspire

In the Tirio Indian village of Kwamala, deep in the Amazon rain forest, Kamanya lay in his hammock, burning with fever. His mother sat nearby fanning him.

"Kamanya, Kamanya," she whispered, but he did not answer. She spoke gently to her husband. "It is time. Take him." He picked up the boy and carried him to the hut of the shaman—the medicine man.

Softly chanting, the shaman Nahtahlah disappeared into the forest. He returned with leaves, roots, and bark, which he put into a pot of water boiling on the fire. Stirring and singing, he asked the sickness to leave the boy. Then Nahtahlah removed the pot from the fire, and when the mixture had cooled he lifted Kamanya's head and poured the warm medicine into the boy's mouth. The shaman's song ended as night came. Kamanya's parents sat beside him until morning. When the boy awoke, the fever was gone.

As the years passed, Kamanya would remember the shaman's ritual as if it were all a dream. But he never forgot that the shaman saved his life.

The village of Kwamala rested on the banks of the beautiful Sipaliwini River. Kamanya's mother and sisters bathed and washed the family's clothes in the river. They grew cotton, which they spun into cloth. And they ground up achiote berries to dye the cloth red.

While his mother and sister harvested cassava root and made it into bread and his father hunted for tapir, Kamanya swam and fished in the river's clean waters and ran free as the wind through the forest with the other boys.

Unlike the other boys, Kamanya often slipped away and silently followed the shaman as he collected the plants from which he made his powerful medicines. Kamanya hoped that he could learn Nahtahlah's wisdom and one day become the next shaman. Nahtahlah was pleased with the boy and showed Kamanya which plants he used for healing.

One day a man from another tribe came down the river. He staggered from his canoe, up the riverbank, and into the Tirio village. He told the Tirios that strangers had come to his people's village in search of gold. These miners had dug up the ground—and they carried a disease so strong that the tribe's shaman could not cure it.

A few days later the man passed on to the spirit world. Soon people in the Tirio village became sick with the strange illness—and Nahtahlah could not cure it.

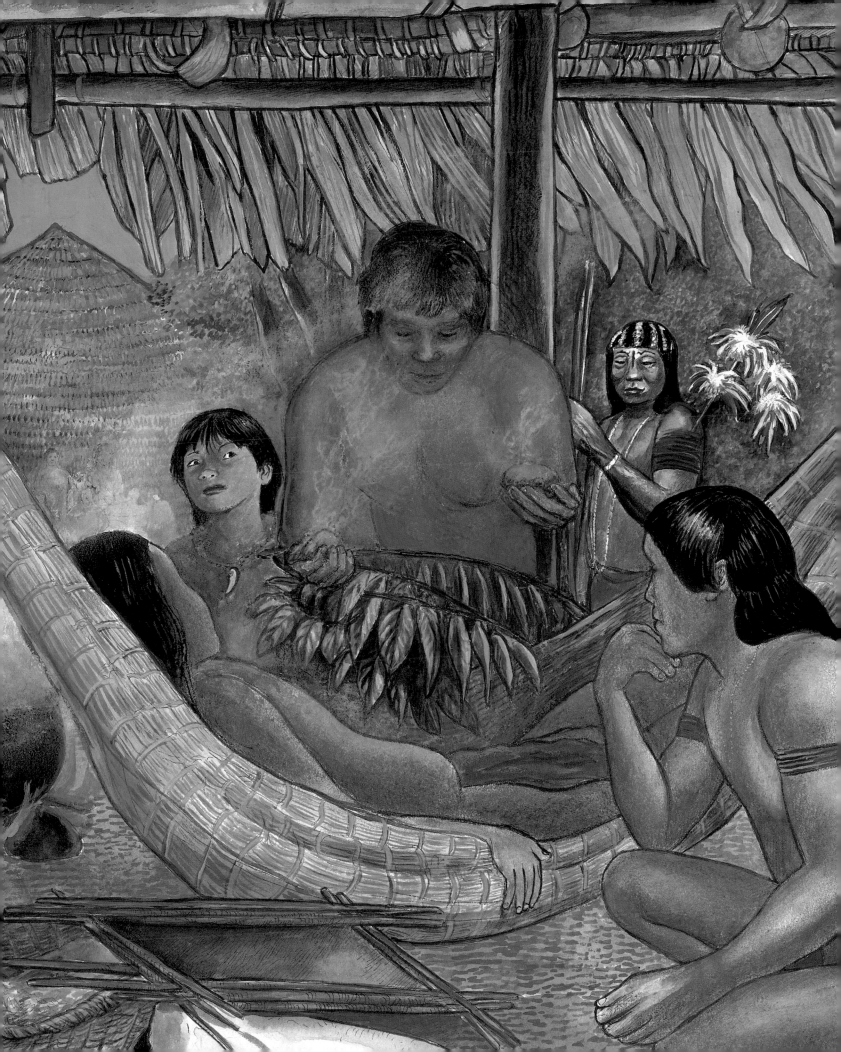

Several months later, another canoe came down the river. The tall people who entered the village had the whitest skin the Tirios had ever seen and hair the color of straw. Their clothes covered their entire bodies. These white people were missionaries who had come to convert the Tirios to their religion. They gave the sick people little white pills, and soon everyone in the village felt well. They called this sickness "malaria" and said the little white pills contained "quinine," malaria's treatment.

The missionaries gave the Tirios new clothes to wear, taught them how to read and write, and translated the Bible into Tirio. And they welcomed traders who arrived in airplanes and exchanged metal pots and pans, rice, and plastic bottles for emerald tree boas, scarlet macaws, and poison dart frogs.

Kamanya watched the forest's wildlife go, in small bamboo cages, down the river and up into the clouds.

Before the missionaries arrived, the Tirios believed in gods who told them to respect the forest that sustained them. But the white people's medicine had done what the shaman's medicine could not. So now the Tirios believed that the missionaries' god must be more powerful than their own gods.

Kamanya watched sadly as the shaman lost his place of honor within the tribe and at the council fire. He told Nahtahlah, "Tamo, Wise One, the day must come when they again see that you are the wisest of them all."

For four years life went on this way. Then the missionaries went away, believing their work complete.

One day while Kamanya was fishing, he saw another stranger coming up the river, a young woman accompanied by a guide from another village. Kamanya brought her to see the chief.

The woman, Gabriela, explained that she had come to study the healing magic of the forest plants. The chief told her about the malaria and asked why she wanted to learn their medicine when hers was so much stronger.

"Do you know where the treatment for malaria comes from?" Gabriela asked. She explained that missionaries had learned about quinine, the medicine in the white pills, from the forest people of Peru. "This healing medicine comes from the bark of the cinchona tree," she said. The chief was astonished. A shaman's medicine had saved them after all.

Every day Gabriela followed the shaman through the forest and learned about the hundreds of plants he used for medicines; plants to cure earaches and stomachaches, snake and insect bites.

One day Nahtahlah noticed Gabriela scratching her elbow. Going over to a *weedee* tree, he peeled the bark away. He spread the bright red sap on Gabriela's arm. By the next day the fungus and itching had disappeared.

After several months Gabriela left. But every year she returned to Kwamala to learn, with Kamanya, more and more of the shaman's wisdom.

Five years had passed since Gabriela's first visit to Kwamala. As the small plane circled over the village, the people streamed from their huts to greet her. When she landed, they carried her bags upon their heads, laughing and smiling, happy to see their friend again.

Now Gabriela could speak effortlessly in their language. And on this visit she had a special gift—a book that she had made for them.

As always, Gabriela went first to call upon the chief. She carefully unwrapped her handbook of all their medicinal plants and said, "Now you have two books in your language—the Bible and this, the wisdom of Nahtahlah. Now your people will never forget the shaman's wisdom. Perhaps one day the people of the world may benefit from Nahtahlah's knowledge of the healing powers of the rain forest."

That night the chief called a meeting of the village elders.

The next day Kamanya visited Gabriela and said, "The chief thinks your book is very important. He has asked Nahtahlah to teach a young man of our tribe all he knows. Nahtahlah has chosen me!"

Gabriela left the Tirio village with a full and happy heart. She would continue to return to Kwamala year after year and learn from her wise mentor. And she knew that while she was away the old shaman's work would continue with Kamanya.

And so it was that Kamanya became the shaman's apprentice.

And so it was that after Nahtahlah passed on to the spirit world, Kamanya became the shaman, patient and wise, who healed his people.

AUTHORS' NOTE

All of the world's cultures use plants and other growing things as medicines. Even in our industrialized society, most of the medicines we use are manufactured from synthetic—man-made—chemicals based on compounds found in natural products. Aspirin, for example, is based on a chemical that came from willow bark; codeine in cough syrup was derived from chemicals in the opium poppy; and penicillin was first extracted from a bread mold. In the more remote corners of the world, such as in the jungles of the Amazon, people have always used the forest as their medicine cabinet. For thousands of years, shamans have passed on the information about the healing properties of rain forest plants from one generation to the next. As forest peoples come into increasing contact with the outside world, however, their traditions are being disrupted as they are led to believe that modern synthetic medicine is always more effective than their own. In many instances, their traditional medicines are as effective as modern medicine and, in some cases, more so. This book tells the story of one tribe who learned the importance of their own knowledge about the healing properties of the rain forest. It is based on a true story that was first told in the book *Tales of the Shaman's Apprentice* (Penguin, 1994).

—L. C. and M. J. P.

CACAO edible
Weh-da-ga

Kah-tam we-mah
for stomach-aches

POKEWEED
Pah-nah-ra-pah-nah

CUSTARD APPLE
for fevers

Ko-noy-uh for coughs

for bee-stings
Ku-run-yeh

IPECAC (leaves)
for fevers

IPECAC (flower)
Ku-ri-lu-eh-nah-pe-da

for aching joints
Ku-pe-de-yuh

HELICONIA for fevers

for ant bites
Neh-da-am-we

CURARE arrow poison
U-rah-re

for stomachaches
Ah-lu-gah-lu-gah

SNAKEWEED
for snake-bites

for fevers
She-tu-u-ru

SPIDER ORCHID

for infections
Uh-kuh-pu-ru

for snake-bites
Ah-kov-pah-tu-puh

THEOBROMA (WILD CACAO)
for fevers
Ah-de-gah-nah-mah

HOG PLUM
Mo-pa edible